Disney's Adventure Stories

Disney PRESS

New York

TABLE OF CONTENTS

TABLE OF CONTENTS

Written by Sarah E. Heller

Designed by Alfred Giuliani

First Edition

1 3 5 7 9 10 8 6 4 2

This book is set in 20-point Cochin.

Library of Congress Catalog Card Number: 00-109918

ISBN: 0-7868-3290-8

For more Disney Press fun, visit www.disneybooks.com

Disney's TARZAN ®

JUNGLE DANGERS

In an African jungle, Tarzan learned to swing from the trees like a monkey. But Tarzan could also do things that none of the gorillas in his family could do. He could swim with the hippos. And he could make things with his hands—like a spear that was as sharp as a

rhino's horn. Tarzan wondered why he was so

different.

One day
when Tarzan
was wrestling
with his best
friend, Terk, the
two tumbled

from the nesting grounds. Suddenly, a leopard jumped

into the clearing! It was Sabor, the gorillas' worst

enemy. Quickly Tarzan and Terk ran back to the

nesting grounds, with Sabor close behind.

"Roar!" Kerchak, the great gorilla leader, beat his chest. Protecting his family, Kerchak threw Sabor, but the leopard attacked again. His sharp claws and teeth injured the great gorilla. Kerchak fell to the ground. He could not get up.

Terrified, the gorillas watched from the trees as the leopard moved in for the kill. But just then, as Sabor leaped at Kerchak, Tarzan swung down on a vine.

With his feet, Tarzan knocked Sabor backward.

Now the leopard was furious!

Snarling and growling, Sabor faced Tarzan.

Tarzan had his spear ready and he lunged at Sabor.

"Rrarooww!" screamed the leopard.

The struggle continued as the two enemies scrambled up into the trees. With lightning speed, they twisted and turned, jumped and flew. Sabor leaped down at Tarzan from above. With the handle of his spear, Tarzan fended off the cat and threw him from the branches.

Bravely, Tarzan jumped from the tree to face Sabor again. The leopard lunged at him, knocking the spearhead off of Tarzan's weapon. As he dodged Sabor's claws, Tarzan saw the spearhead in some underbrush and dove for it. Sabor dove in after him.

A hush fell over the gorilla family. Terk

watched and waited, fearing for her friend. Then, at last, Tarzan climbed out of the underbrush, holding Sabor's limp body. He let out a cry of victory.

"OO-oo-oo, ah-ah-ah!" cheered the gorilla family,

but Kerchak did not join them. The big gorilla turned

sadly and began to walk away. He felt he had failed to

protect his family.

With a solemn

face, Tarzan

approached his

leader. Then he

laid the leopard at

Kerchak's feet

as a sign of respect. As Kerchak looked at Tarzan,

a new sound thundered through the jungle.

Bang! Bang! Gunshots blasted nearby. Quickly,

Kerchak ordered the gorillas to retreat to safety. Tarzan

started to move with them, then changed his mind. He

was curious. Climbing high in the trees, he followed the

new sound.

What are these creatures? thought Tarzan, as he

looked

down at

three

humans.

They did

not look like any animal he knew. He followed the one

with the funny yellow fur. She was running after a

young baboon. Pieces of paper fell from her hands.

Tarzan picked one up. It was a drawing of the baboon.

Suddenly, Tarzan heard the strange yellow-furred

creature yell. A group of angry baboons was chasing her!

Swooping down on a vine, Tarzan grabbed the

creature. They sailed through the jungle with the baboons

close behind. The yellow animal kicked at the monkeys. She carried a strange sort of stick that opened. What an interesting weapon, thought Tarzan.

Now he surfed along on the mossy branches of the highest trees. Baboons raced at them from all directions. Tarzan slid into a hollow trunk. The baboons slid in after them.

Suddenly they were all falling, tumbling through the air.

"Ahhh!" screamed the creature in Tarzan's arms. He held her with one hand and grabbed for a vine with the other. Tarzan struggled to hold on. Gently, he placed the creature safely on a tree branch.

Baboons fell past them, all but two. The young

baboon and his mother floated down, using the creature's funny stick as a parachute. The young baboon wanted the piece

of paper that was stuck to the creature's fur. Tarzan grabbed it and handed it to him.

Then he turned to the animal that had caused all of

T A R Z A N

the trouble. She was a funny-looking creature. Moving closer, Tarzan stared at her face. It was smooth like his. Their eyes looked the same.

Tarzan was puzzled. He looked harder. The creature

 did not have fur, after all. Instead she was wearing fancy yellow cloth. He was surprised to see that she had two

legs like his, with toes like his. Beneath the white

material on her hands were long thin fingers. Tarzan

put his own

hand against

hers. They were

the same!

Now Tarzan

knew the truth.

There were

other creatures like him!

"Tarzan," he grunted, pointing to himself.

"I'm Jane," said the girl.

With wonder and joy, Tarzan took her hand. At last,
he felt he had a place in the world.

Disney's POOH'S GRAND ADVENTURE

The Search For Christopher Robin

THE RESCUE PARTY

"It's a quest, is it?" cried Owl excitedly. "A long and dangerous journey through the Vast Un-Nown!"

"Dangerous?" squeaked Piglet. The friends huddled together.

As Owl told of woozles, jagulars, and the mighty

Skullasaurus, they
became terrified.

Pooh had shown
Owl the note that
Christopher Robin had
left for him that
morning. It was terrible
news! Christopher
Robin was in trouble.

He was in a place called . . . *Skull*! Owl pulled out his
map and pointed to Skull Cave.

They had to rescue him! Pooh, Piglet, Eeyore, Rabbit, and Tigger formed the search party. The friends walked across the bridge and entered the Vast Un-Nown. But before Owl saw them off, he gave his friends an impressive-looking map to help them find

their way. Unfortunately, none of them was quite sure that they could read it.

Nonetheless, the rescue party found its way through the dark and scary Forest of Thorns, and on into the

Valley of Flowers. Here the sun shone, a stream bubbled, and friendly butterflies lifted Piglet into the air.

"Oh, d-d-dear!" cried Piglet. He was terribly

afraid of heights.

Quickly Pooh hopped onto a log and grabbed Piglet's foot. Up, up, into the sky they went, until the butterflies began to let go and fly away.

"Oh bother," said Pooh.

Crash! Piglet and Pooh landed in a heap.

Rabbit was not happy. He decided to take charge.
They had to follow the map! It was the only way to find
Christopher Robin. And so the group continued on, with
Rabbit leading the way. They were doing fine until the
map ripped on a branch. Half of it floated away on a
breeze.

"After

that map!"

cried

Tigger,

bouncing

off after the piece of paper.

Before long, Tigger had bounced himself right onto a log between two cliffs. Far below was a river. With a gasp, Tigger hugged the tree trunk for dear life.

Then, suddenly, the log began to fall!

The friends rushed over and grabbed Tigger, but they could not hold on. With a splash, they all fell into the shallow water below.

Shaking the
mud from their
ears, they
continued on.
It became very
foggy. Rabbit
hung his head.
They were lost.

Feeling tired and defeated, the friends settled down
to sleep. Only Pooh stayed awake. Without
Christopher Robin, he felt empty. He didn't know how

to be happy without his best friend.

In the morning, the friends realized that they were closer to their destination than they had thought. In front of them was Skull Cave! Inside there were echoey

noises, dark shadows, and mysterious crystals that made things look strange. There were also many paths, and before long, Pooh got separated from the others.

"Rumble, grumble, ROAR!" came a terrifying

sound. Piglet looked at his friends sadly. They all

thought that the Skullasaurus had gotten Pooh.

"Roar!" went the monster again. Over time,

the growls grew more fierce. Suddenly a scary shadow

loomed over them. Then, out stepped . . .

"Christopher Robin!" cried the friends.

The boy smiled at the group. He had been searching for them everywhere.

"We're so very glad to see you!" cried Piglet. The

friends all started to tell Christopher Robin of their adventure.

Then Christopher Robin explained the truth. He had not been missing at all. He had been at *school*, not Skull. Now the boy wanted to tell Pooh all about it.

"Oh, Christopher Robin!" cried Piglet. "He was gobbled up by the Skullasaurus!"

"The what?" asked the boy. Just then, a loud growl echoed from the cavern. Christopher Robin began to laugh. "That's no Skullasaurus," he told them. "That's the rumbling tummy of a hungry-for-honey Pooh Bear!"

Sure enough,
when Christopher
Robin lowered a
pot full of honey
into a nearby
cavern, he pulled
up one very sticky
bear! Pooh was so

happy that he threw his arms around his friend.

"Silly old bear!" Christopher Robin laughed, twirling
Pooh around.

Hand in hand, Pooh and Christopher Robin walked home with their friends. In their hearts, they would always be together—forever and ever.

ROBIN HOOD

A Hero with a Heart of Gold

For a long time, Robin Hood and Little John had lived like bandits. But they were guilty of only one crime: they stole from the rich to give to the poor. The Sheriff of Nottingham took everything from the people as taxes for greedy Prince John. Only Robin and Little John kept the people's hopes alive and kept food on

their tables.

Robin
and Little
John had
a trunk full
of disguises,
and they

were very good at tricking Prince John and the sheriff.

One morning, they dressed like fortune-tellers and

stopped the royal coach. They ran off with the prince's

gold and jewels before he realized what was happening!

Of course, this made Prince John furious. He wanted

to catch the outlaws, so he set a trap. He announced

that a great archery tournament would be held at the

castle, knowing that Robin Hood would not be able to

resist. Robin was the best archer in the land. And the

winner would get a kiss from the lovely Maid Marian.

And so, disguised as a stork, Robin entered the

competition.

Little

John had

also devised

a clever

disguise. He

wanted to

be at the tournament to see his friend win. Disguised as Sir Reginald, the Duke of Chutney, Little John walked straight to the royal box and took a seat—right next to Prince John!

Before long, Robin Hood was well on his way to winning. Even when his competitor, the sheriff, tried to cheat, Robin's skill was so great that he could not be beat.

"Hooray!" cheered the crowd when the stork won the contest. In the royal box, Maid Marian stood and clapped. No disguise could fool her. She knew that the best archer in the land was her sweetheart. She loved

Robin Hood with all her heart.

"Bravo!" said Prince John. But as the stork bowed

before him, the prince ripped his costume with a sword.

The archer's true identity was revealed!

Quickly, the prince's guards surrounded Robin Hood.

But with Little John's help, the outlaw soon managed to

free himself. Little John threw him a sword. Together,

the two friends fought off the guards. While Robin

dodged arrows and clashed swords, he swept Maid

Marian off her feet. "Marian, my love, will you

marry me?" Robin Hood asked.

"Oh, darling, I thought you would never ask me,"

answered Maid Marian with a smile.

They escaped to Sherwood Forest, and there, among

waterfalls and fireflies, Robin gave Marian a ring made

from a flower. All night they danced and sang with their

friends. Everyone in Nottingham was happy; everyone except Prince John.

"Triple the taxes!" ordered the angry prince.

The sheriff was only too happy to collect more money.

Those who couldn't pay went to jail. Even good Friar Tuck was taken to prison and sentenced to death! How could Robin Hood save his friends now? The prince was just

waiting for him to attempt a rescue.

Robin Hood needed another great disguise. Dressed

as one of the guards, he slipped into the castle. Not even the sheriff knew that Robin Hood had entered the castle grounds.

Then, when the coast was clear,

Robin Hood
signaled to
Little John,
and the two
outlaws
made their
way into the

castle jail. While Little John freed the prisoners,
Robin found the gold that the sheriff had collected
from the townsfolk. He was almost finished sliding
the treasure bags to Little John when Sir Hiss, the

prince's adviser, saw him.

Before long, all of the guards came running, and the sheriff was hot on Robin's tail.

"Get going! Don't worry about me," Robin said to

Little John and the freed prisoners.

The sheriff chased Robin into the castle tower. His

eyes burned with anger. He did not like to be tricked.
With a blazing torch, the sheriff set the tower on fire.
There was only one way to escape.

Bravely, Robin Hood jumped into the moat far
below. His friends watched nervously from the shore,

hoping that Robin Hood was all right. Quickly,

he swam to safety.

Soon the whole kingdom was rejoicing. Robin

Hood was a hero, and good King Richard had

returned to rule the land. At their wedding, Robin Hood and Maid Marian sealed their future together. It was a day of peace and joy in Nottingham.

THE DRIVE TO SURVIVE

A ladar was not like other dinosaurs. Before he had even hatched, his egg was stolen from its iguanodon nest, dropped into a river, and seized by a

giant pteranodon. Then, as it sailed over the ocean, other flying dinosaurs attacked. The egg fell and landed in a leafy tree on an island just off the mainland.

The lemurs that lived on the island had never seen a dinosaur egg before. Cautiously, Plio approached it. The egg started to crack! A cute and helpless baby dinosaur crawled out and into her arms.

For many years Aladar lived on Lemur Island. He

grew into a large, strong iguanodon. His life with the

lemurs was peaceful and happy. Aladar knew nothing

about his dinosaur relatives on the mainland.

Then, one day, everything changed when a meteor hit the earth! As flames showered down around them, Aladar and his lemur family raced to safety. Leaping from a cliff, they fell into the raging ocean water below. When his lemur family was safely on his back,

Aladar swam across the sea to the mainland.

Cautiously, the family explored the unfamiliar land.

Then, slowly but steadily, the earth began to tremble.

They had run into a giant herd of leaf-eating dinosaurs!

"Stay out of my way!" shouted a giant iguanodon named Kron. Marching around Aladar and the lemurs were dinosaurs of all shapes and sizes. One dinosaur, Baylene, was so enormous that she stepped easily over Aladar. Little dinosaurs hurried to keep up with the

Herd. No one wanted to be left behind.

Joining the Herd,

Aladar and the lemurs learned that Kron was leading them to the Nesting Grounds. It was a place with plenty of food and water. "It's the most beautiful place there is. . . ." said Eema, an old styracosaur. But Kron was pushing the Herd too hard.

Aladar asked Kron to slow down for those who were having trouble. But he would

not listen. For days the Herd marched across a hot
desert. Still, Kron pushed them faster.

Finally
the Herd
reached a
lake bed,
but there
was no
water.

"Keep moving," said Kron, but Eema sat down,
exhausted. Aladar and Baylene ran to help.

Thump! Thump! Baylene's enormous feet thundered in the lake bed.

"Lift your foot, Baylene!" called Aladar.

There was water pooled in Baylene's footprint!

Soon all of the dinosaurs came running for a drink.

"Wait! Wait! There's enough for everyone," Aladar said. But they all pushed and shoved. Two orphan dinosaurs were so scared that they hid. It wasn't until nightfall that Aladar could help the little ones get a drink.

Kron's sister, Neera, had been watching Aladar. She wondered why he was always looking out for others. As she stood talking to Aladar at the lake bed, Kron's

lieutenant, Bruton, came charging over the ridge. He was badly wounded. "Carnotaurs!" he cried.

Kron ordered the Herd to run. But Eema and Baylene did not have the strength to keep up. They were going to be left behind. Aladar and Neera wanted

to help them, but Kron pushed his sister forward. "Stay

away from him!" he ordered her.

Soon the Herd was far away. Baylene, Eema,

Bruton, Aladar, and the lemurs were on their own.

Carefully, Aladar coaxed the wounded Bruton into a

 cave for the night.
Plio gently nursed
his cuts. Then the
sound of footsteps
approached. The

vicious carnotaurs had arrived. "Save yourself!" Bruton told Aladar. As the iguanodon pushed his friends farther into the cave, Bruton bravely fought the carnotaurs. Aladar wanted to help, but Bruton slammed into the cave wall, causing part of the cave to collapse.

"Bruton!" cried Aladar, but it was too late. The brave warrior had been crushed along with his enemies.

Sadly, the others walked farther into the cave, looking for another way out. "Do you smell that?" asked Zini the lemur. The other lemurs sniffed the air and pulled at a few stones. Small points of sunlight appeared through cracks in the rock! The dinosaurs pushed at the rocks. At last, the wall gave way!

Beyond the wall was paradise. It was the Nesting Grounds! Lush green trees and soft grass were

everywhere. But the Herd had not arrived yet. A landslide blocked the old entrance.

Determined, Aladar went back through the cave and set out to find the Herd. He found them trying to climb over the landslide. "There's a safer way!" he called to the Herd, but Kron angrily knocked Aladar to the

ground.
Neera knew
that Aladar
needed help.
As she
joined the
fight, Kron

backed away.

Just then, a carnotaur appeared. "Stand together!"

Aladar shouted to the Herd. The group intimidated the

carnotaur. It hesitated until it noticed one dinosaur off

by itself. It turned and climbed after Kron.

Neera scrambled up the rocks to help her brother, but it was too late. Now the carnotaur came after her. Quickly Aladar knocked the meat-eater away from Neera. With a roar, the carnotaur fell from the cliff.

At last, the Herd was free to finish the journey. When Aladar led them to their new home, the dinosaurs bellowed happily. Neera rubbed her neck against Aladar's. He had been right all along. By standing together, they had survived.

WALT DISNEY
PICTURES PRESENTS

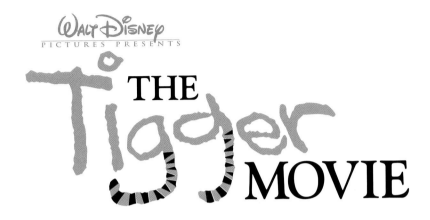

THE Tigger MOVIE

The Search for Tiggers

Roo was worried about Tigger. All day the two of them had been trying to find Tigger's family. They searched high and low through the Hundred-Acre Wood for Tigger's family tree, but every one of the large and stripedy trees was empty. When they

looked for clues at Tigger's house, all they found was a

locket with no picture inside. Then they had tried

writing a letter. For hours, Roo and Tigger had waited

by the mailbox. No tiggers had shown up, and no letters

had come in reply. When the sun set and Roo had to leave, Tigger was very sad and lonely.

"I would do anything to make him happy again,"

Roo told Kanga.

Roo loved Tigger like a brother. He loved to bounce and play with him. Just that day, Tigger had shown Roo how to do a very special

bounce. He wished that he and Tigger were family.

"But Roo, dear," said Kanga, "Tigger *is* one of our family." In all of the ways that counted, he sure was.

All of Tigger's friends felt the same way. They wanted to cheer him up, so they decided to answer his letter. They each added their own heartfelt thoughts. Then Owl signed it: "Your family."

When Tigger read the letter, he thought it was from  his tigger family. He was sure they would come for a visit! He began cleaning, decorating, baking, and planning for a

tigger family reunion.

His

friends

were very

worried.

They

knew that

it would

break Tigger's heart if his family did not show up. So

they made costumes and dressed like tiggers.

"Come in! Come in! Come in!" cried Tigger.

"There's lotsa catchin' uppin' we gotta do!"

There was cake, and music, and bouncing. In the

excitement, Roo tried to do the special bounce that

Tigger had taught him. With a *bing, bang, boom,* Roo

crashed into the closet and his mask came loose. Tigger

stared in surprise, realizing that these were his friends

in costume. He was hurt to think they were playing

a joke on him.

"Somewhere out there, there's a *real* Tigger family!" said Tigger. He took the letter and locket and stood by the open door. Wind and snow blew in and swirled around him. "So T-T-F-E. Ta-Ta-For-*Ever*!"

Before his friends could tell Tigger the truth about the letter, he was gone. For hours he stomped through the snow looking for tiggers. It was cold and windy. He was about to give up, when all of a sudden there appeared before him the most gigantical, snow-stripedy tree he had ever seen! Tigger was sure this was the tigger family tree.

"Halloo up there!" he called. "Is anybody home?"

Tigger bounced right into the branches. But there were

no other tiggers in the tigger family tree.

Then Tigger saw something down below. Could it be

his family? No, it was Roo and Pooh and the rest of his

friends. They had been searching for him all night.

Suddenly, the ground began to shake. Snow was

roaring

toward

them. It

was an

avalanche!

Quickly

Tigger

bounced his friends to the safety of the high tree

branches, but he could not save himself. The rushing

snow swept Tigger away.

"Tigger!" cried Roo. He could not lose Tigger now!

Roo twisted his tail. He wound up his leg. He got into

position and . . . wow! Roo sailed through the air. He

saved Tigger from the crashing snow and together they

bounced all the way back to the tree.

Tigger praised his little friend. "What a Whoop-de-Doopin' Loop-de-Loopin' Alley-Oopin' Bounce *that* was!" he cried proudly.

"It was, wasn't it?" said Roo.

Then the friends explained about the letter.

"Ya mean, you fellows are my family?" Tigger asked in surprise.

"I'm afraid we have nothing better to offer," said Pooh.

Tigger smiled at them. He realized that they really were his  family in all the ways that count. "I shoulda seen it all along," said Tigger.

He was so happy that he threw a giant party to celebrate when they got home. Christopher Robin even took a picture for the locket, and Tigger gave the

locket to Roo.

"Only the best for my *bestest* little brother!"

said Tigger.

Walt Disney's

Peter Pan

PIRATE DREAMS

Late one night, high above the city of London, a figure dressed in green soared across the starry sky. It was Peter Pan! Along with him flew his trusted friend, a small pixie named Tinker Bell.

Together, Peter and Tinker Bell landed just outside the Darling family's nursery window. Inside, Wendy, John, and Michael were fast asleep. Peter sneaked in without a sound and began to look for his shadow. He had left it

behind the last time he had come to visit the nursery— and he had to get it back.

"Must be here somewhere," he said to Tinker Bell. He found it inside a dresser drawer, but it flew away. Peter began to chase the shadow around the room. When he accidentally knocked over a small table, the noise woke Wendy—and soon Michael and John were up, too.

Before long, Peter had convinced the children to

come back with him to Never Land. "But Peter, how do we get to Never Land?" Wendy asked.

"Fly, of course," Peter answered. Peter gave the children a flying lesson. "All you have to do is . . . is to . . . Huh! That's funny," Peter said. "It's just that I never thought of it before. Say, that's it: you think a wonderful thought!"

Then Tinker Bell sprinkled pixie dust over them. In no
time at all, the children were flying through the nursery
window and out into the night sky. Peter Pan led the
way around Big Ben, the giant clock tower of London.

Then they headed for the second star to the right and straight on until morning. At last, they looked down from the air to see a beautiful island.

"Oh, look! There's Cap'n Hook and the pirates!" cried Michael, pointing down below. Sure enough,

Michael had spotted Captain Hook's ship.

But Captain Hook had also spotted them. He wanted

nothing more than to
blast that annoying
Peter Pan right out of
the sky. So he ordered
all hands on deck and
shot a cannonball
straight at Peter and
the children.

Whizzz! Luckily, the
cannonball missed them. But Captain Hook was not

finished yet! He got ready to fire another shot.

Peter Pan stayed behind to draw Hook's fire while
Tinker Bell led the children down to the island. But
Tinker Bell was flying so fast, the children could not

keep up. In fact, Tinker Bell was trying to leave them behind. She was very jealous of Wendy. So she raced ahead to Peter's hideout. There, she told the Lost Boys that Peter Pan wanted them to shoot at Wendy. They took aim with their slingshots and soon a shower of

stones flew toward Wendy. She lost control and began to fall out of the sky!

Just then, Peter Pan swooped down from out of nowhere and caught her. "Oh, Peter, you saved my life!" she cried. Tinker Bell went red with jealousy.

When everyone was safely on the ground, Peter Pan introduced the children to the Lost Boys. Then, as Michael, John, and the Lost

Boys went off to explore the island, Peter Pan took

Wendy to Mermaid Lagoon. There they found a few

mermaids sitting on the rocks at the foot of a waterfall.

While the mermaids tried to convince Wendy to come

in for a swim, Peter heard a sound. It was a faint

ticktocking—like the sound of the crocodile that was

always following Captain Hook!

The mermaids dove into the water in fear. But Peter

and Wendy flew off toward the sound and trailed

Captain Hook to Skull Rock. He was with his first

mate, Smee.

They had

kidnapped

the Indian

princess,

Tiger Lily.

"You tell me the hiding place of Peter Pan," Captain Hook said to Tiger Lily, "and I shall set you free."

But Tiger Lily refused to reveal the secret. Peter Pan had to save her. Otherwise, Hook would leave her tied up in the watery cave. When the tide came in, Tiger Lily would drown!

Before long, Peter and Captain Hook were locked in a duel. Peter thought it was great fun. He landed on Hook's blade. He flew around him. Finally, Peter Pan lured the pirate off a rocky ledge. At the last minute, Captain Hook managed to grab the ledge with his

hook. But suddenly the rock gave way, and he splashed

down into the water. He was chased away by the crocodile.

In the nick of time, Peter Pan rescued Tiger Lily and flew her back to the Indian camp. The

Indian Chief was so grateful, he gave Peter the name "Chief Little Flying Eagle."

It was only the first of many adventures that Wendy and her brothers  would have with Peter Pan. And when it was time to go home, Peter sailed them through the sky and back to

London on a magical golden ship. The Darling children left Never Land far behind, but their memories of the wondrous place stayed with them forever.

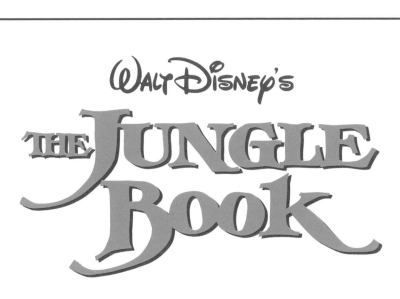

Walt Disney's THE JUNGLE BOOK

HEART OF THE JUNGLE

Mowgli had lived with the wolves since he was a tiny baby. He howled, scratched, and wrestled with the wolf pups. The jungle was his home. But as Mowgli grew, his wolf parents worried for his safety. The tiger, Shere Khan, had sworn to kill the boy.

The tiger was afraid of man's guns and man's fire, and he feared Mowgli

would grow up to be a hunter. For Mowgli's

protection, the wolves thought it best for him to go to

live in the Man-village with his own kind.

One day, a friend came to the wolves' den. It was

Bagheera, the panther. He was the one who had found

Mowgli alone in the jungle when he was just a baby.

Bagheera took Mowgli for a long walk. When night came on, Mowgli yawned. "I'm getting a little sleepy," he said. "Shouldn't we start back home?"

"Mowgli, this time we're not going back," said Bagheera. "I'm taking you to the Man-village. Shere Khan has returned to this part of the jungle." Bagheera did not think it was safe for Mowgli to stay. But Mowgli did not care.

As Bagheera drifted off to sleep in a tree, a snake named Kaa slithered through the leaves. "Go away!"

Mowgli told the python, but Kaa was hungry. He
looked deeply into Mowgli's eyes, hypnotizing him.
Then he started to wrap his tail around the boy!

Just then, Bagheera opened his eyes. "Kaa!" cried

Bagheera. Startled,
the snake hit his
head on a branch,
and Mowgli snapped
out of the trance.
Then the boy shoved
the snake out of the

tree. Mowgli laughed as Kaa skulked away with a knot in his tail.

But Bagheera was troubled. "So you can look after yourself, can you?" he said angrily to Mowgli. He was worried for the boy.

Later that night, Mowgli ran away from the panther. I *can* take care of myself, he thought. Luckily, Mowgli was not alone in the dangerous jungle for long. He met a friendly bear named Baloo.

"Hey, kid, you need help," said the bear, "and old Baloo's gonna learn you to fight like a bear." And so

he did. Soon Mowgli and Baloo were laughing and
playing like old friends. They ate bananas and
scratched their backs. Then, floating down the river,
they hummed a happy tune.

Suddenly, dozens of orangutans swung down from the trees. They grabbed Mowgli and tossed him around. "Give me back my Man-cub!" cried Baloo. The orangutans liked to play. They dangled Mowgli by his toes and threw fruit at Baloo.

"Bagheeeerrrraaa!" roared Baloo, calling for the

panther's help.

But the orangutans escaped into

the jungle with the Man-cub. They brought Mowgli to their leader, King Louie. He sat on his throne inside some ancient ruins. He promised to help Mowgli stay in the jungle if the boy would teach him how to make fire.

The orangutan king swung Mowgli around the

temple, and a party began. Everyone started dancing to the beat. Then a mysterious new orangutan joined the

group. She really knew how to move. But as King Louie danced with her, her costume fell to the ground. It was Baloo!

King Louie grabbed Mowgli and ran. Baloo and Bagheera raced

after him. Swinging around a column, Baloo knocked some stones loose. *Crumble, rumble, crash!* The ancient ruins were falling down! In the commotion, Mowgli escaped on Bagheera's back.

"Ha! Ha! Ha!" said Baloo when they were safe. "Man, that's what I call a *swinging* party!"

The next morning, Baloo woke Mowgli early. As they traveled through

the jungle, Mowgli could tell something was wrong.

"What's the matter, old Papa Bear?" asked the boy.

Sadly, Baloo explained. As much as Baloo loved Mowgli, he knew he could not keep the boy safe from Shere Khan. Mowgli belonged in the Man-village.

"The Man-village!" cried Mowgli. "You're just like old Bagheera!"

Feeling betrayed, Mowgli ran away again.

He ran until he couldn't hear Baloo calling him anymore. Then Mowgli sat down and

started to cry. A group of vultures tried to cheer him up.

Then, all of a sudden, the frightened vultures flew to a high tree branch. "Run, friend, run!" the birds cried to Mowgli.

Out of the jungle bounded Shere Khan! He was

after Mowgli! But Baloo had caught up just in time. He

grabbed the tiger by his tail. Around and around they

ran. Finally, Shere Khan broke loose. He was furious!

With his sharp claws bared, the tiger attacked Baloo.

Nearby, thunder roared and lightning flashed. A tree

burst into
flame.
Mowgli
grabbed a
burning
branch and
tied it to
Shere Khan's

tail. The mighty tiger ran away in fear, and the vultures

cheered for the Man-cub.

Later, as Mowgli hugged Baloo, they heard a strange

sound. It was singing—a girl singing. Mowgli had never seen a human before. He was mesmerized! When the girl smiled at him, Mowgli went with her and followed her to the Man-village.

As Mowgli looked back to say good-bye, he knew Baloo and Bagheera were right: this was the way it should be. He had found his real home. But the jungle—and his jungle friends—would always remain in his heart.

Too Much Nonsense!

Alice was distracted as she sat in the tree, listening to her sister read from her history book. "If I had a world of my own, everything would be nonsense," Alice

said to her kitten, Dinah. Alice began to imagine a place without facts or figures or boring history lessons.

Alice took Dinah on a little walk through the daisies. Suddenly a rabbit with white fur hopped by. He was wearing clothes and carrying a pocket watch—and talking to himself! "I'm late! I'm late!" he cried. Alice stared in surprise. Then, even though she knew it wasn't sensible, she hurried after the White Rabbit.

When he ducked into a rabbit hole, Alice crawled in after him. Inside, it was dark and cramped, and Alice couldn't quite see where she was going. Then, before she knew it, the ground beneath her was gone, and Alice was falling!

"Good-bye, Dinah!" she called to her kitten. It was a long, long way down, but Alice wasn't frightened. Her skirt billowed out like a parachute, and she slowly floated down. When she finally reached the bottom, she

did not have a bump or a scratch on her.

"Oh, Mr. Rabbit!" called Alice. Soon she managed

to exit the dark hole and enter a whole different world.

She was still looking for the White Rabbit, but instead,

she met a pair of twins named Tweedledee and

Tweedledum. They shook Alice's hand and told her a

nonsensical story. Alice loved it, but she was in such a

rush to find the White Rabbit, she didn't have time to

stay for another.

Hurrying down a path, she came upon a pretty little house. Upstairs were some cookies and a little sign that said, EAT ME. So Alice helped herself.

Suddenly she felt funny. Her feet crashed through the walls. Her arms grew out the windows. Alice had become a giant!

What would she do now? "Perhaps if I ate

something, it would make me grow smaller. . . ." said

Alice. With one bite of a carrot, Alice grew so small

that she had trouble climbing down the stairs.

Soon tiny Alice found herself in a garden. The flowers were singing a lovely song about the beautiful afternoon. The rose, violets, and lilies welcomed Alice warmly until a haughty orchid called her a weed.

"I'm not a weed!" cried Alice, but the flowers pushed her away roughly.

They did
not want
her to stay
and take
root.

Angrily,
Alice
walked away through the tall grass. A while later, she

spotted a smiling animal sitting in the trees. At first

Alice could only see his toothy grin. Then some stripes

appeared, and finally a face.

At last she saw that he was a cat! Alice confessed to him that she was beginning to grow tired of all the nonsense. But the Cheshire Cat said, "Most everyone's mad, here." Then he pointed the way down a path and disappeared.

Taking the path pointed out by the Cheshire Cat, Alice soon wandered into a tea party. The March Hare and the Mad Hatter were singing a merry song. Alice

was delighted to learn that they were celebrating their

*un*birthdays, because it was *her* unbirthday, too. She sat

down to join them, but they kept changing seats and

taking her cup away. "Of all the silly nonsense, this is the stupidest tea party I've ever been to in all my life!" Alice said as she walked away.

In the depths of Tulgey Wood, unusual creatures peered at her. Alice sat down and started to cry. Before long, a familiar smile lit up the darkness.

"Oh, Cheshire Cat!"

cried

Alice. "I

want to

go home,

but I

can't find

my way."

"That's because you have no way," said the cat. "All

ways here are the *Queen's* way!"

With that, a tunnel magically appeared in the tree

trunk. Alice hurried through it and found herself in a

maze of hedges. Playing cards were painting the roses

red. When Alice asked why, they said they had planted

white roses by mistake. If the Queen of Hearts found

out, they would surely lose their heads.

"Goodness!" said Alice. She took a paintbrush and started to help them. Then a trumpet blasted, and the playing cards lined up to make way for the Queen.

The White Rabbit came running, announcing Her Majesty.

It was not long before the temperamental Queen

was annoyed with Alice. "Off with her head!" cried

the Queen of Hearts, pointing at her.

Alice ran for her life. The Queen chased her back

to the Mad Hatter's tea party. Suddenly everything seemed so big.

"I can't stop now," said Alice.

"But we insist you must join us for a cup of tea," the March Hare replied. Soon, he, the Mad Hatter, and Alice all fell into a giant cup of tea. Alice swirled around and around until she found herself swimming in an ocean. Then, out of nowhere, a little door appeared before her. Alice ran to it, but it was locked.

"I simply must get out!" she cried.

"But you *are* outside," the Doorknob told her.

Alice peeked through the keyhole. There, on the

other side, she saw herself, asleep under a tree.

"Please wake up, Alice!" she cried, and suddenly her

eyes opened. There was Dinah sitting on her lap. After all that nonsense, her sister's history book looked very inviting. Alice took her sister's hand and walked home. They were just in time for tea.

FRIENDS TO THE RESCUE!

Nothing seemed to be going Woody's way. First, his arm had torn, and he couldn't go with Andy to Cowboy Camp. Then, he had fallen off the dog while rescuing a toy penguin from the yard sale Andy's mom was having. And now, Woody had been toynapped! A

toy collector named Al had stuffed Woody inside his bag and driven away!

Back in Andy's
room, the toys
planned a rescue
mission. They
recognized Al from
the TV commercial
for his toy store.

"To Al's Toy Barn and beyond!" called Buzz Lightyear.

The toys walked through the neighborhood all night.
Finally, they spotted the toy store across a busy street
with fast-moving cars. They needed a way to cross.

"There must be a safe way. . . ." said Buzz. Then he had an idea. Hiding under bright orange traffic cones, the friends inched their way across the road.

Inside the store, there were aisles and aisles of toys.

The group decided to split up to look for Woody.

Buzz found an aisle of space rangers. Hundreds of

Buzz Lightyears filled the shelves! Buzz wanted to

get a better look. But as he climbed onto the shelf, one of the new space rangers attacked him.

"All space rangers are supposed to be in hyper-sleep until awakened by authorized personnel," said the new Buzz. The two began to wrestle. Soon Andy's Buzz was being twist-tied into a cardboard Buzz box.

"Let me go!" he cried, but it was no use. The rest of the toys had

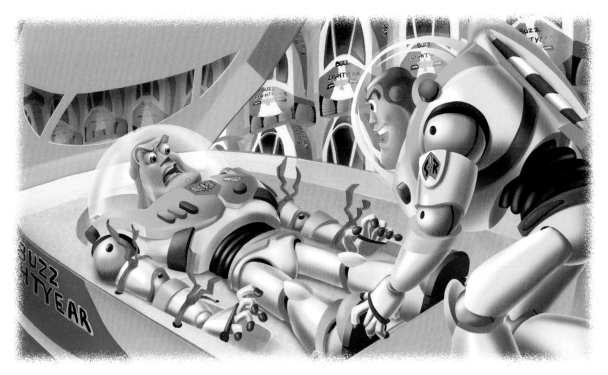

pulled up in a toy car. They thought the new Buzz

was Andy's Buzz. The new Buzz hopped into the

car, and they all headed for Al's office.

"No, no, guys! You've got the wrong Buzz!" cried

 the real Buzz Lightyear. But the others couldn't hear him! Finally, he pushed at his box—*crash!*—and managed to escape when it fell over.

Meanwhile, the toys found Al in his office and sneaked into Al's bag, hoping he would take them to Woody. Buzz saw Al headed for the door and realized his friends were in Al's bag.

Quickly, the space ranger jumped on a trampoline, grabbed a hanging toy, and flew across the store on a zip line. But the door closed just as Buzz reached it. Desperately, Buzz toppled a pile of toys onto the electric mat that controlled the door. When it opened,

Buzz ran after Al.

In Al's high-rise apartment, Buzz found

his friends and Woody. Everyone looked at the two Buzz Lightyears in surprise. "So who's the real Buzz?" asked Woody.

Just then, Andy's Buzz lifted his foot and showed them Andy's name written on the bottom. Then Buzz turned to Woody, ready to take him home to Andy's house. But the cowboy did not want to be rescued.

Woody had discovered that he was a highly valuable collectible. In the 1950s, there had been a TV show called *Woody's Roundup*. Now the whole TV gang was together again! There was Jessie the cowgirl, Bullseye the horse, and a mint-in-the-box Prospector doll. Al was selling the whole set to a museum in Japan.

Woody knew that Andy would grow up. What would happen

to Woody then? In a museum, he could live forever.

"Woody," said Buzz, trying to convince his pal to come home, "the point is being there for Andy when *he* needs us!" But Woody had made up his mind to stay with the Roundup toys.

Sadly, Buzz turned his back and walked away,

ducking into an air vent along with the rest of Andy's toys.

"Buzz! Buzz!"

cried Woody. "Wait! I'm coming with you!" He had realized that his friend was right. A child's love was

more important than anything. Buzz heard Woody call after him, and he turned to go back for his friend. But it was too late. The Prospector stood in Woody's way. He wanted to go to the museum, and for that to happen, the Roundup gang had to be complete. Then,

Al came home. He packed Woody and the Roundup

gang into a green case and headed for the elevator.

Buzz and the rescue team needed to save Woody!

Charging down the air duct, the friends found their way

outside. Quickly, they raced after Al, but they couldn't

catch up. He was headed for the airport. The toys

would need a car to save Woody now.

There by the curb was a Pizza Planet truck, still

running. Climbing in through the open door, Buzz took

control of the steering wheel. Slinky hit the gas. Rex told

Buzz which way to go. It was a scary ride, but the toys

made it to the airport just in time.

Hiding in a pet carrier, the rescue team caught up

with the green case containing the Roundup toys. Buzz

lifted the lid. Woody and Bullseye managed to escape,

but the Prospector was fighting mad. Andy's toys were

ready. They found a camera in some baggage, and

using the flash, they blinded the Prospector. Then

Woody and Buzz sent him flying inside a little girl's backpack.

Unfortunately, Jessie was still stuck in Al's suitcase! She was being loaded onto the airplane. Woody and

Buzz raced after her on Bullseye's back. It was their

most daring rescue yet! Woody climbed into the cargo

hold and pulled Jessie free. Then, just as the plane

started to move, Buzz rode Bullseye alongside the plane.

Woody and Jessie jumped to safety.

"Yee-hah!" they cried. Now they could all go home together to Andy's house, where they could be real toys—played with and loved by a real kid.

The Girl Who Saved China

C hina was under attack by the Huns! The Emperor's counsel rode into Mulan's village to spread the news. "One man from every family must serve in the Imperial Army!" he announced.

Mulan had no brothers, so her father would have to

go. But he was weak and had already served his country in battle. Mulan knew that her

father would not survive
another war.

So that night, Mulan
cut her hair short like a
man's. She took her
father's armor and his
sword. Then, as her
family slept, she galloped
off on her horse, Khan.
At the army training
camp, she reported for

duty, calling herself Ping and pretending to be a man.

At first, "Ping" had a difficult time at training camp.
Captain Shang gave all of the recruits long poles to use
as weapons. But Mulan could not get the hang of it.

She kept getting tripped up, and she failed the exercise miserably.

Next, Shang had the troops carry heavy weights to build their strength. As hard as she tried, Mulan could not keep up. Finally she collapsed on the ground, exhausted. Captain Shang ordered her to go home.

Disgraced, Mulan turned to leave. Then, in the center of camp, Mulan spotted an arrow at the top of a pole. Captain Shang had put it there as a challenge to the recruits: they had to climb the pole and get the arrow with a heavy disk tied to each wrist. Each of the soldiers

had tried and failed. But Mulan decided to give it one last try.

This was her last chance to prove herself.

She studied the disks carefully. Then, wrapping them together, she

used their weight for balance as she shimmied up the pole. The troops cheered! Even Shang grew to respect the strange soldier.

When it was time for the recruits to join the army in

battle, Mulan was ready. Shang and his troops

marched to the front line to meet another battalion.

But instead they met with disaster. The other battalion

had been defeated by the Huns.

"We're the only hope for the Emperor now," said Shang.

As they marched, a rocket inside the munitions wagon exploded. The sound of the explosion led the Huns right to them! Showers of arrows rained down on the army. Quickly Mulan raced to her horse, Khan. She untied him

just before the entire wagon went up in flames.

Now Shang's troops fired their cannons at the Huns. *Boom!* But they were outnumbered. Soon they were almost out of ammunition.

"Hold the last cannon," ordered Captain Shang. He

told the soldiers to aim the cannon at the Hun leader,

Shan-Yu. But Mulan had another idea. She grabbed

the cannon and fired at a snowy mountain peak. Snow

thundered down! A rushing avalanche buried the entire

Hun army—but now the snow was bearing down on

Shang!

Mulan jumped on her horse and pulled Shang from a wave of snow. She had defeated the entire Hun army and saved her captain's life!

But none of that mattered once Shang discovered

Ping was a *woman*. He rounded up his troops and marched away to the Imperial Palace without her. As Mulan sat by a small fire, trying to keep warm, she saw Shan-Yu and some of his army rise from out of the snow. They were alive! And they were headed for the Imperial City.

Mulan raced to the city. The victory celebration was beginning. There would

be fireworks and other festivities. Mulan had to warn
Shang before it was too late. "The Huns are alive!" she
said to him. "They're here." But neither Shang nor
anyone else would listen to her.

Frustrated, Mulan watched as the Huns invaded the

city and captured the Emperor in the Imperial

Palace. The soldiers tried to break down the palace

door, but it was no use.

"I've got an idea!" shouted Mulan. Three of the

soldiers followed her. She disguised them as women.

Then, using the trick Mulan had demonstrated at camp,

they shimmied up the palace pillars. Even Captain

Shang joined them once he understood Mulan's plan.

Inside the palace, the Huns were easy to overtake. They did not expect women to attack them! As Shang battled Shan-Yu, the soldiers rescued the Emperor. Mulan stayed behind to help Shang.

"The soldier from the mountains!" Shan-Yu cried when he recognized Mulan. In a rage, Shan-Yu raced after Mulan, leaving Captain Shang

behind. Mulan lured him onto the palace roof. Shan-Yu thrust his sword at her. But Mulan used her fan to block his blows and twist the sword out of his hand.

At that moment, a rocket from the fireworks tower

was headed for Shan-Yu. He tried to get out of the way,

but Mulan pinned his cloak to the roof. Then she jumped

clear. In a great explosion, Shan-Yu was gone forever.

Now even the Emperor bowed to Mulan, the girl who had saved all of China. With honor, she returned home a hero, finally free to be herself.

Walt Disney
PICTURES PRESENTS

THE RESCUERS DOWN UNDER

Journey Through the Outback

In a classy New York restaurant, two little mice named Bernard and Miss Bianca were having an elegant dinner together. In Bernard's pocket was a beautiful ring. He was planning to ask the lovely Miss Bianca to be his bride.

But before Bernard could propose, the mice were summoned by the Rescue Aid Society. Bernard and Miss Bianca were needed in Australia at once. A little boy named Cody had been  kidnapped by a mean animal poacher and was locked up in a cage!

Quickly the two little mice set out on their journey.
On the back of Wilbur the albatross, they flew
through an icy snowstorm and around the world. They
had made many daring rescues before, but they had
never traveled this far from home.

The Australian landscape was barren. Dry desert

and scrub spread to
the horizon. Which
way should they go
to find Cody?

Luckily, Bernard

and Bianca had found a friend: a rugged kangaroo mouse named Jake. He knew the outback better than anyone else. "So, which way are you taking—Suicide Trail through Nightmare Canyon, or Satan's Ridge?"

Bernard gulped nervously and looked at his map. "A

map's no good," said Jake. "What you need is someone

who knows the territory." And so Jake became their guide. He began by rounding up their first ride — on the back of a flying squirrel! Then the three mice sailed down a river on the back of a python. And when the python could not go on, they continued their journey on the backs of lightning bugs.

Miss Bianca could not bear to think of poor little Cody trapped in a cage. The mean poacher, Percival McLeach, had been trapping wild animals for years and selling them for money. But what could he want with a little boy?

Finally the mice reached the McLeach compound. As they watched from the shadows, a huge steel door began to open.

"Get out of here! Get!" cried McLeach. He shoved Cody out the door. "It's all over! Your bird is dead."

"No!" cried Cody. The golden eagle, Marahute, was

 his friend.

The poacher's eyes gleamed with evil. "Too bad about those

eggs," said McLeach. "They'll never survive without their mother."

Cody turned and ran into the outback. The mice watched as McLeach started his big truck, the bushwacker, and prepared to follow Cody. They knew this must be some kind of trick.

Quickly the mice jumped into the truck. It rumbled

along to a high cliff. They could see Cody climbing to the eagle's nest, just as McLeach had expected. He had lied to Cody about having killed Marahute so he could find out where the eagle's nest was.

As fast as their little legs would carry them, the

mice climbed after Cody. "You're in great danger!"

cried Bianca. Startled, Cody turned toward the mice.

They pointed to McLeach.

Just then, the golden eagle flew into the canyon.

"Marahute, turn back!" cried Cody, but it was too late.

As McLeach trapped the golden eagle in midair in a large sack, Cody jumped from the cliff to save his friend. Jake lassoed the boy's foot. He and Bianca held on to the rope and were carried along with Cody. But Bernard did not reach the rope in time. He watched as his friends were lowered into the cage of the bushwacker along with Cody and the eagle.

Bernard ran after them. He

was beginning to think he would never catch up when

he came upon a wild boar. Climbing on its back,

Bernard rode the

boar through the

outback.

At last,

Bernard spotted

the bushwacker

near Croc Falls. McLeach had tied Cody to the crane

of the bushwacker and was lowering him into the

river. Hungry crocodiles waited in the water below.

Quickly, Bernard hopped into the truck and grabbed the keys. The crane stopped, but Cody was still dangling over the water.

"Look, it's Bernard!" cried Bianca from inside the cage. Bernard threw the keys to Bianca so she and Jake could free themselves and Marahute. Meanwhile, McLeach's pet lizard, Joanna, spotted Bernard. The little mouse ran full speed toward McLeach as Joanna

chased after him. *Boom!* The lizard collided with

McLeach, and the two of them—the poacher and the

lizard—fell into the river.

Just then, the rope that held Cody snapped.

"Bernard!"
cried Miss
Bianca. "The
boy!" Bernard
spotted Cody
and leaped into

the water to try to save him. But the current was too

strong for them.

"Noooo!" cried McLeach as he plummeted over the

thundering waterfall. Bernard and Cody were close

behind. The boy and the mouse were carried over the

falls and

tumbled

through the

air. Then, all

of a sudden,

they were

going up, not down! They found themselves on Marahute's back, along with Miss Bianca and Jake. The eagle had swooped down and saved them!

Cody hugged the great eagle, and Bianca hugged Bernard. "Oh, Bernard, you are magnificent!" she cried. As they flew away on the golden eagle, Bernard reached into his pocket. He finally asked Bianca to marry him, and she said yes. One thing was certain: their life together would be one big adventure!

WALT DISNEP
PICTURES PRESENTS

THE EMPEROR'S NEW GROOVE

THE EMPEROR AND THE PEASANT

Once upon a time there lived a selfish young emperor named Kuzco. He had plans to destroy an entire peasant village just so he could build his own

fabulous summer getaway, Kuzcotopia.

Pacha, one of the peasants who lived in the village, was summoned to the palace to learn about Emperor Kuzco's plans. Pacha was terribly

upset. "What will I tell the village and my family?" he

wondered. Downhearted, he loaded his cart and set off

for home.

When he arrived, Pacha noticed a strange sack on his cart. It was moving! And inside was a talking llama—a

very *rude* talking llama! Pacha was shocked when he discovered that the creature was Emperor Kuzco himself.

"What happened?" Pacha asked, pointing to the emperor's new hooves.

Kuzco looked down and screamed in horror. Until that very moment, he had not realized what had happened to him. His adviser, Yzma, had tried to poison him, but had accidentally changed him into a llama instead!

Remembering none of this and not knowing he had

enemies at the palace, the emperor demanded that

Pacha return him to his home. The peasant refused.

Unless the emperor would agree to build Kuzcotopia

somewhere else,

Pacha would not

help him find his

way back.

Angrily, the

stubborn llama

strutted off into

the jungle alone.
Pacha called out
after him, shouting
warnings about
jaguars, snakes,
and quicksand.
But Kuzco paid no

attention. Before long, he had accidentally awakened a

pack of sleeping jaguars.

Kuzco took off with the jaguars hot on his heels.

Lucky for him, the kindhearted Pacha had followed

Kuzco, knowing the emperor would never survive in the jungle on his own. So, just when it looked as if all hope was lost for the emperor, Pacha swung in on a vine, rescuing Kuzco from some hungry jaguars. But then the vine wrapped itself around a high tree branch until Pacha and Kuzco were tied down tight.

And that was only the beginning of their troubles. *Crack!* The branch broke under their weight! Still tied to the branch, Pacha and Kuzco bounced down the mountain and into a rushing river. They tumbled and bobbed in the fast-flowing water. Then they sailed

over a roaring waterfall and fell into the swirling mist below. The fall snapped the vines, and Pacha was able to wriggle free and pull

the unconscious Kuzco to the riverbank.

That night, Pacha tried once more to convince

Kuzco to cancel his plans to destroy his village. But

even after Pacha had saved his life, Kuzco refused.

"Unless you change your mind, I'm not taking you

back," said Pacha.

The next morning, the

emperor seemed to have

a change of heart. He

suggested that he might not

destroy Pacha's village after

all. Pacha believed him. So he shook Kuzco's hoof and

led him on through the jungle.

"Follow me,"

said Pacha,

starting across

an old bridge.

Suddenly, the

floorboards

collapsed. Pacha fell through the hole, getting tangled

in a rope. "Help!" Pacha shouted, but Kuzco did

nothing to save him. He had lied and was still actually

planning to do away with Pacha's village.

Then the floorboards gave way beneath the llama.
Now he was tangled in the rope, just like Pacha. Pacha
and Kuzco dangled over the canyon and got into a
punching and kicking brawl over the lie Kuzco had

told

Pacha.

Crack!
The

bridge

broke in

half and the ropes

snapped. They tumbled

down, but ended up

wedged together in a

tight crevice. Pacha

showed Kuzco how

they could work

together to inch their

way up the gorge, back-

to-back. But then, as Pacha reached for a dangling

rope that would save them, the llama began to slip.

"Kuzco!" cried Pacha. He grabbed the llama by the tail. Somehow, in a frantic scramble, the llama and the peasant had reached the top of the cliff. But in the blink of an eye, the rocky ledge began to crumble beneath their feet. Just in time, Kuzco pulled Pacha backward and onto safer ground.

In disbelief, Pacha stared at the llama. "You just

saved my life," he said. "I knew that there was some good in you." From that point on, Pacha and Kuzco were a team. They raced to the palace and, working together, they defeated Yzma and found the antidote that turned Kuzco back into his human form.

Through the course of Kuzco's adventure, he had learned about life, friendship, and how to treat people. He became a better leader. He also realized he had been wrong: Pacha's village didn't need Kuzcotopia, because it was perfect just the way it was. Kuzco enjoyed visiting his new friends in the village, and the whole kingdom enjoyed having a more compassionate ruler.

FLIK FIGHTS FOR FREEDOM

Flik was headed for The City. He had promised the ant colony that he would find some big bugs to help them fight Hopper and his gang of grasshoppers. Every year, the grasshoppers forced the ants to gather food for them. But this year, just before the grasshoppers arrived, Flik had knocked over the offering stone, and all of the grain had been

lost! Now the grasshoppers were demanding double their usual order!

Determined to stop the bullies, Flik hiked to the edge of Ant Island. Then, hanging on to a dandelion puff, he flew across the canyon of a dried-up riverbed. Most of the ants thought they had seen the last of Flik, including Princess Atta, whom Flik most wanted to impress. But Atta's little sister,

Dot, waved as Flik sailed away. She thought he was special.

Flik reached the other side of the canyon and marched into The City. Bugs of all shapes and sizes crawled and flew around him. Flik knew he had come to the right place. He was sure to find some warrior bugs here.

At a bug bar inside an old paint can, Flik noticed

some rough-looking flies. He moved closer for a better

look and saw a ladybug challenging them and using one

of his friends, a walking-stick, as a sword! Was there

going to be a fight? Flik got pushed aside by other

onlookers and couldn't see. Suddenly the ladybug and

his friends ran up the wall of the paint can. The whole

bug bar rolled and crashed. The next thing Flik knew,

the ladybug and his friends were standing on top of the

flies. Along with Francis the ladybug and Slim the

walking-stick,
there was Rosie
the spider, Dim
the beetle, the pill
bugs Tuck and
Roll, Manny the
praying mantis,

Heimlich the caterpillar, and a moth named Gypsy. Together, they made quite a group.

"Wow! You're perfect!" cried Flik. "I've been scouting for bugs with your exact talents!" He couldn't believe his great luck. In no time at all, the warriors had agreed to come back with him to Ant Island. Boy,

would Princess Atta be surprised! But when Flik arrived with his strange crew, Princess Atta was nervous. Would they be able to fight Hopper?

She was right to be nervous. As soon as Rosie found

out that Flik thought they were warriors, she told him the truth: the city bugs were circus performers.

Oh no! thought Flik. If the other ants found out, they would never forgive him. Desperately, Flik begged the circus bugs to stay. "Please, please don't go!"

Suddenly a big bird's head peeked over the rocks.

Terrified, the bugs scattered in different directions. No

one noticed little Princess Dot in the sky above, clinging

to a dandelion

puff. She had

been following

Flik and was

copying his

flying trick.

"Squawk!" The bird flew after Dot. She screamed,

but Francis was on his way. He flew to Dot and saved

her, catching the little ant in his arms. Then they both tumbled into a crack in the riverbed.

Peck, peck. The bird tried to pull them out with her beak and knocked some stones into the crack. One of them broke Francis's leg! Another one knocked him out! Flik had to do something. While Heimlich and Slim distracted the bird, Flik and the circus bugs flew to the

rescue. Using Rosie's
spiderweb, they carried
Dot and Francis to safety.

"Hooray!" cried the
ants. Even Princess Atta
trusted Flik after seeing
the bravery of the city
bugs. She helped organize
the colony to work on
Flik's big plan: to make
a fake bird to scare Hopper away.

The ants worked long and hard, putting all their efforts into building the bird out of sticks and colorful leaves. When the project was finished, everyone celebrated. They all believed that Flik's plan could work.

Whirrr! Suddenly, the frightening sound of approaching grasshoppers filled the air. When Hopper saw that there was no food waiting for them, he landed and angrily grabbed the Queen.

"Not one ant sleeps until we get every scrap of food on this island!" cried Hopper.

Only Flik could save them now. Climbing inside the fake bird, Flik swooped down upon the bullies. Below, the circus bugs created fake blood from berry juice. They pretended that the bird had hurt them.

It was working! The grasshoppers began to run

away. Even
Hopper was
frightened—
until the bird
caught fire
and Flik had

to make an emergency landing. Now Hopper knew

that it wasn't a real bird!

"You are mindless, soil-shoving losers put on this

earth to serve us!" Hopper yelled at the ants.

"No," said Flik. "Ants don't serve grasshoppers. It is

you who need *us*! We're a lot stronger than you say.

And you know it, don't you?"

Angrily, Hopper knocked Flik to the ground. But

the brave ant stood up again.

Hopper and the grasshoppers looked around. Hundreds of angry ants glared back at them. They realized they were outnumbered. Suddenly the entire colony rushed at the grasshoppers.

Hopper grabbed Flik and flew away. "Flik!" cried Princess Atta. Giant raindrops began to fall. Quickly Atta flew to help her friend, dodging the raindrops.

At last, Atta caught up and grabbed Flik. Hopper
chased them with fury as Flik and Atta led him
straight to a bird's nest.

"Another of your bird tricks?" Hopper asked. He didn't know it was a real bird this time. With one last look of surprise, Hopper realized that the ants had led him to his doom.

Now the colony was free. By banding together, they had chased the grasshoppers away. All of the ants agreed that Flik was a big hero.

DISNEY's

THE
GREAT MOUSE
DETECTIVE

BASIL SAVES THE DAY

Dr. David Q. Dawson had traveled to London for the celebration of Queen Moustoria's sixtieth year on the throne. On a rainy night in the great city, the doctor wandered through the streets, looking for a room to rent. Suddenly he heard the sound of weeping.

He followed the sound and found a young mouse in tears, sitting in a dark corner. Dr. Dawson hurried over to her aid.

The little mouse's name was Olivia Flaversham. "I'm trying to find Basil of Baker Street," she explained. She handed Dr. Dawson a newspaper clipping of an article about the Great Mouse Detective.

"I don't know any Basil," said Dr. Dawson, "but I do know where Baker Street is." Together, they found the home of Basil of Baker Street. There, little Olivia told her story to the detective. Her father, a kind and gentle toy maker, had been taken—by a bat with a peg leg!

Basil knew the creature well. It was Fidget, the

assistant to his worst enemy, Professor Ratigan. "Who

knows what dastardly scheme that villain may be

plotting, even as we speak!" exclaimed Basil.

Later that evening,

the terrifying face of

the bat appeared in

the window! Basil

and Dr. Dawson

raced outside. Fidget

was gone, but the mice found his hat lying in the street.

It was just the clue they needed to track Fidget. The

detective found his friend, Toby, a basset hound. Toby

sniffed the hat and carried

the mice through the

streets of London to a

toy shop.

Inside, dolls, games,

and toys were piled to the

ceiling. Basil noticed that some mechanical parts were

missing from some of the toys. What had Fidget been

up to here? And what kind of evil scheme was

Ratigan plotting?

It was dark and quiet. Olivia did not realize the

danger she was in. She wandered over to a pretty

doll cradle. Curious, she peeked inside.

Suddenly, Fidget jumped out at her. He stuffed

Olivia into a bag and raced toward a window in the

roof. Basil tried to give chase, but a pile of toys tripped

him up. The bat had gotten away with Olivia.

Basil paced around the toy shop, thinking hard.

Then Dawson pulled out a piece of paper that he had

discovered earlier. Fidget had left it behind. Back at
Basil's house, they did several experiments and found
that the paper had salt water and coal dust on it. *Aha!*
Ratigan's hideout had to be near the riverfront!

Dressed in disguises, Basil and Dawson made their
way to a tavern near the harbor. Before long, Basil

spotted Fidget.
Quickly, Basil and
Dr. Dawson
followed him
through a series of

drainage pipes
to Ratigan's
secret lair.

"Surprise!"
yelled Ratigan
and his men.

Basil had walked right into his trap.

Ratigan tied down Basil and Dawson in a

mousetrap. All around them were deadly contraptions

rigged to a record player. When the song ended, the

mice would be doomed!

"It was my fond hope to stay and witness your final scene," said Ratigan, "but you *were* fifteen minutes late, and I do have an important engagement at Buckingham Palace." As Ratigan flew off in a blimp, Basil began to think hard. He calculated the angles and the timing of the trap. By setting it off early, the mice were soon free!

Without a moment to lose, they found Olivia and

raced to Buckingham Palace after Ratigan. There they

discovered what he was up to. With the toy parts

Fidget had stolen, Ratigan had forced Olivia's father,

the toy maker, to build a robot that looked and talked

just like Queen Moustoria! Then Ratigan had captured

the real

queen.

Now there

was a huge

crowd

listening to the robot queen. The robot was telling the queen's subjects that she was naming a new royal consort—Ratigan!

But Basil arrived just in time. He gained control of the robot queen and used it to foil Ratigan's plan. Then

Basil rushed onstage and yelled, "Arrest that fiend!"

The angry crowd chased

after Ratigan, but he snatched Olivia and flew away in his blimp. Basil, Dawson, and Olivia's father

made their own hot-air balloon out of balloons, a flag, and a matchbox. They rose up into the sky and chased Ratigan.

Bravely, Basil jumped onto Ratigan's blimp just as it

crashed into Big Ben, the giant clock tower. Ratigan, with Basil and Olivia right behind him, scrambled into the tower, dodging the clock's enormous gears. Basil shoved Ratigan's cape into the clockwork, trapping him. Then Basil picked Olivia up and raced away, intent on getting her out of harm's way. Just as Basil was delivering Olivia safely to her father, Ratigan

reappeared and jumped at him. Basil and Ratigan both

tumbled down through the air.

They landed on the giant hands of the clock, and

Ratigan came at Basil once again. He knocked Basil

from the

hands, but

as Basil

fell, he

grabbed

ahold of

the blimp wreckage. Basil hung on for dear life.

BONG! BONG! The clock chimed the hour. The

minute hand moved, and Ratigan lost his balance. As

he fell through the air, he grabbed at Basil's foot. The

rope that Basil was hanging from snapped under their

weight. Down they fell toward the city below, carrying

some of the blimp wreckage with them.

Olivia started to cry, but then a faint sound gave her

new hope. Hooray! There was Basil, soaring up toward them, using the propeller of the blimp as a pedal-powered helicopter. The Great Mouse Detective had saved himself—and saved the day once again!

DISNEY's
Aladdin
AND THE
KING of THIEVES

A TREASURE LOST, A TREASURE FOUND

Aladdin could not believe the news he had just heard from the Oracle. His father was alive!

Princess Jasmine and Aladdin were to be wed, but Jasmine encouraged him to go find his father. "Take as long as you need," she said.

Aladdin hugged the princess. "I'll be back in time for our wedding. I promise."

The

Oracle had

told him

that his

father was

with the

Forty Thieves. Thinking that his father was their

prisoner, Aladdin flew off on the Magic Carpet with

Abu and Iago and picked up the trail of the thieves.

He caught up with them at the edge of the sea.

Aladdin held back and watched from a safe distance.

"Open, sesame!" cried their leader. Suddenly the waters parted like magic, and the thieves rode through on their horses. Just before the waves crashed in again, Aladdin sneaked in behind them.

On the other side of the water, Aladdin found himself

in the thieves' secret lair. But he could not stay hidden. Before long, Aladdin and the King of Thieves were standing face-to-face. It was his father, Cassim! He was not the thieves' prisoner—he was their leader!

Cassim was shocked to see his son. The rest of the thieves were outraged.

"The boy is an intruder!" cried Sa'Luk. The menacing

thief wore sharp, golden claws on his hand. "And we have rules about intruders. He must die!"

Cassim did not want Aladdin to be killed, but he could not appear weak in front of his men. He knew that Aladdin had only one chance for survival. "My

son should face the Challenge," he said. Aladdin would have

to face Sa'Luk in a battle to the death. The thief was

strong, but Aladdin was smart and quick. He dodged

Sa'Luk's sharp claws and tried to defend himself. Even

when the foes battled their way onto a dangerous cliff

ledge, Aladdin did not back down. Finally, Sa'Luk lost

his balance and fell into the water below.

Cassim smiled proudly. Aladdin had faced the

Challenge and won. Now he was officially a member of the Forty Thieves.

Later that night, Cassim told his long-lost son of a great treasure that he was seeking. It was called the Hand of Midas, and everything it touched turned to solid gold.

Aladdin was angry. So this was the reason that his

father had not been a part of his life. All through Aladdin's childhood, Cassim had been off searching for treasure.

Cassim tried to explain himself to his son. "I knew exactly what I wanted for my family—the best."

"We never wanted gold. We wanted you," Aladdin said. "I wanted a father. I still do. Come to my wedding."

Cassim did come back to the palace with Aladdin. But it was only to get his hands on the Oracle. He hoped the magical staff could tell him where to find the priceless treasure, the Hand of Midas. When Aladdin found out about his father's motives, he was hurt and

angry. He sent his father off with the Oracle to find his treasure, and said good-bye, hoping that Cassim was

out of his life forever.

But then Aladdin learned from Iago the parrot that Cassim was in trouble. Sa'Luk was alive! He had turned against Cassim and taken him captive. Aladdin knew he had to help. Cassim may have turned his back on his family, but Aladdin would not make the same mistake.

So, with Jasmine, the Genie, Iago, and Abu, Aladdin flew off on the Magic Carpet to rescue his father. "The Vanishing Isle!" gasped Aladdin. A beautiful island rose out of the sea on the back of a great turtle. It was the home of the Hand of Midas. Sa'Luk had taken the

Oracle from Cassim and used it to find the treasure.

Aladdin found his father and Sa'Luk in the city on the Isle. Jumping from a nearby rooftop, Aladdin knocked Sa'Luk to the ground. He and Cassim got away and found the temple that contained the Hand of

Midas. All of a sudden, there was water rushing at them. The great turtle was diving, and soon the

Vanishing Isle would be under water. Together,
Aladdin and Cassim climbed to the Hand of Midas!

"Be careful," Cassim warned Aladdin. "Don't
touch the Golden Hand!"

Aladdin carefully threw the treasure to his father,

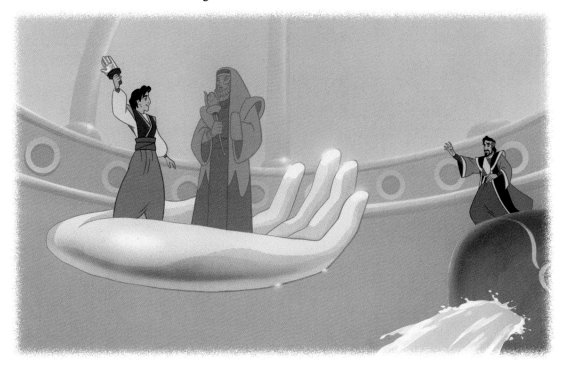

and Cassim caught it in his robe. Instantly, the cloth turned to gold.

But Sa'Luk had caught up with them, and he had Aladdin trapped. "Give the Hand of Midas to me, Cassim," Sa'Luk ordered, "or your son dies!"

Cassim threw the treasure to his enemy. Sa'Luk caught it in

his hands. The
greedy thief
became a golden
statue. He fell
like a stone into
the water.

Aladdin and Cassim carefully recovered the treasure
and scrambled to escape the rising water. When they
were safe, the King of Thieves took one last look at the
Hand of Midas.

"This wretched thing almost cost me the ultimate

treasure," said Cassim. He hugged Aladdin. "It's you, son. You are my ultimate treasure. I'm sorry it took me this long to realize it." Then he threw the Hand of Midas away. Together, Cassim and Aladdin returned to Agrabah to celebrate the wedding as a family—at last.

Disney's
THE BLACK CAULDRON

DEFEAT OF THE HORNED KING

The evil Horned King was after the Black Cauldron! The Cauldron's dark powers would make him invincible. But where was the mysterious Cauldron? The king had captured Hen Wen, a pig with special powers, thinking she had the answer. But Taran,

the assistant pigkeeper who cared for Hen Wen, had managed to free his pig, and she had escaped the wicked king.

Now Taran and his new friend, Princess Eilonwy, were trying to escape from a dark dungeon in the king's castle where they were imprisoned. They wandered through a maze of underground tunnels. When they came to an ancient burial chamber, something gleaming caught Taran's eye.

It was a sword! Taran had always dreamed of being a

great warrior, so he picked up the sword and took it

with him.

Then the

children heard a cry

for help. Following

the sound, they

came upon a kind

old minstrel named Fflewddur Fflam, held captive in

another dungeon. As they began to free him, they heard

the king's henchmen out in the passageway. They were

after Taran and Eilonwy! The three fugitives ran to find an exit and got separated in the commotion.

"Get them!" cried the king's henchmen. One of them cornered Taran. But when Taran's sword touched the henchman's ax, the ax fell to pieces. The sword was

magic! Princess Eilonwy found Taran, and they ran for the castle drawbridge. Using the power of the magic sword, Taran opened the drawbridge, and they escaped across the bridge to the safety of the woods beyond, with Fflewddur close behind them.

At last, they could stop and rest. Suddenly, a furry

little creature tackled Fflewddur, looking for food. It was

Taran's friend Gurgi. He knew that Taran's pig, Hen

Wen, was lost in the woods. "Saw piggy's tracks,"

Gurgi said to

Taran. "Today!"

The group

followed Hen

Wen's footprints

to a lake. When

Gurgi hopped onto some rocks in the water, a whirlpool

began to swirl around him. It was so strong that all four

of them — Gurgi, Taran, Eilonwy, and Fflewddur — were

pulled under. As if in a dream, they soon found themselves in an underground world. It was the land of tiny fairylike creatures called the Fairfolk.

"Hello," said Eidilleg, king of the Fairfolk. "Can I be of any service?" The king was kind to the visitors—but, best of all, Taran found Hen Wen safe and sound among the Fairfolk!

"Oh, Hen!" cried Taran. Hen Wen happily jumped into the boy's arms.

Then the travelers told King Eidilleg of the Horned King's evil plans. King Eidilleg wanted to help. If Taran and

his friends could destroy the Cauldron before the Horned King found it, they could stop him.

King Eidilleg knew where the Cauldron was hidden. So he sprinkled the travelers with fairy dust and sent them off to find it.

The friends soon arrived at a tumbledown cottage. Inside lived three witches, guardians of the Black Cauldron. They were not going to give it up easily.

Taran held out his magic sword. "I offer my dearest possession in exchange for the Black Cauldron," he said.

The witches loved a bargain. They grabbed the sword greedily as the ground began to shake. Then the mighty Black Cauldron rose from beneath the earth.

"Quick! We must destroy it!" cried Taran. But it seemed indestructible.

The witches looked on and cackled wickedly. "The Black Cauldron can never be destroyed," said one of them. "Only its evil powers can be stopped."

"Then there is a way," said Taran. "But how?"

"A living being must jump into it of his own free

will," replied the witch Orddu. Then she added, "However, the poor duckling will never come out alive."

What would Taran and his friends do now? As they sat around a campfire, trying to think of something, flying creatures called Gwythaints flew overhead. Quickly, Gurgi hid behind a tree. The Horned King's

henchmen had found them! The wicked creatures grabbed the

Black Cauldron and took it to the Horned King's castle
along with Taran, Eilonwy, and Fflewddur.

Trembling, Gurgi made his way to the castle. He
was terrified, but he knew he could not abandon his
friends in that evil place. Already the Horned King had
used the Black Cauldron to bring his evil army of
skeletons to life. The army marched out of the castle,

but Gurgi
sneaked past
them and found
his friends.

"Good boy, Gurgi!" cried Taran as the furry creature untied them all. The friends were happy to be rescued. Still, Taran knew they would not be safe — as long as

the Cauldron's

powers were

intact. To protect

the land, Taran

prepared to jump

into the bubbling

Cauldron. But little Gurgi jumped first.

"No!" cried Taran. But Gurgi was gone. The

Horned King's evil army collapsed and the king was

pulled into the Black Cauldron.

As the castle walls crashed down around them,

Taran, Eilonwy, and Fflewddur managed to escape

onto the lake in a boat. Then, from a distance, they watched the castle crumble into ruin. The Black Cauldron appeared, bobbing in the water, and they sadly thought of poor little Gurgi.

The three witches were watching, too. They wanted the Black Cauldron back, and they were prepared to bargain for it. They offered Taran the magic sword in exchange for the Cauldron, but Taran said no.

"I would trade the Cauldron for Gurgi," said Taran.

Immediately, the witches began to fly in a circle.

Wind swept the water like a tornado. When it

stopped, the Cauldron was gone, and Gurgi was lying

on the beach. He reached a

small paw toward Taran.

"Gurgi," cried

Taran, "you're alive!"

With joy, Taran

and Eilonwy hugged

their hero.

"Gurgi's happy day!" said the little creature with a smile. It *was* a happy day—for Gurgi, for his friends, and for all the land.

Disney's
HERCULES

WONDER BOY

All day and into the night, Hercules had traveled toward the temple of Zeus. He had a feeling that the god could tell him about his past. Now, inside the temple, he stood before the giant statue of Zeus.

Suddenly it
started to move!
A great stone
hand reached
down and
scooped him up.

"Didn't know
you had a famous father, did you?" Zeus said with a
laugh. "Surprise!"

Sadly, Zeus explained that when Hercules was just a
baby, he had been stolen and turned into a human.

Hercules' superhuman strength was the only godlike quality he still had.

"If you can prove yourself a true hero on earth, your  godhood will be restored," said Zeus. "Seek out Philoctetes, the trainer of heroes." With that, Zeus snapped his fingers, and a winged horse appeared in the temple.

"Pegasus!" cried Hercules. He remembered playing with Pegasus as a baby.

That night, Hercules and his horse flew to Philoctetes' home on the Isle of Idra. Phil trained Hercules to throw

daggers and swords, and rescue damsels in distress, using a doll for practice. Finally, it was time to test Hercules' strength in the real world. On Pegasus, Hercules and Phil flew toward the city of Thebes.

On the way, they heard a cry for help. Following the

sound, they found a centaur holding a girl in his powerful grip. Hercules rushed to save her. Using his massive strength, he rammed the beast

with his head. The centaur crashed into a waterfall. Then Hercules sent the creature flying with a forceful punch.

The lovely Megara was impressed. "So, did they give

you a name along with all of those *rippling pectorals*?"

she asked.

Hercules stumbled over his words. He felt weak all

over. As he watched Meg walk away, a silly grin came over his face. "Uhhh . . . I'm . . . uh . . . Hercules!"

"I think I prefer 'Wonder Boy,'" Meg replied.

"Isn't she . . . *something*?" Hercules swooned, but Phil was not happy. He thought a hero shouldn't have any distractions.

They flew on to Thebes, a city prone to disaster.
Hercules looked around, eager for a chance to be a
hero. Suddenly, there was Meg, running through the
crowd. "Wonder Boy! Hercules! Thank goodness!"
She told Hercules that two boys were trapped in

a rockslide.

Poor

Hercules! He

didn't realize

Meg was

setting him

up. She had

been sent by Hades, evil lord of the Underworld.

Rushing to save the boys, Hercules lifted a giant

boulder and freed the children from a cave. He did not

realize that the boys were really Hades' minions, Pain

and Panic!
But there
was no time
for him to
find out —
something else

was emerging from a nearby cave. It was a terrible

monster called the Hydra. With gnashing teeth, it came

after Hercules.

Hercules slashed at the monster with his sword. But

when he cut off its head, many more grew back. The

more he cut, the more hideous heads appeared! Soon there were hundreds! Hercules did not give up. He banged his powerful fist into the rocky cliff. Huge boulders tumbled down, killing the monster.

Soon Hercules was famous in Thebes. But he still could not return to Olympus.

"Being famous isn't the same thing as being a true hero," said Zeus. "Look inside your heart."

It did not take

Hercules long to follow

his father's advice. As

he and Meg spent

more time together,

they began to fall in

love. Little did

Hercules know that

Meg worked for Hades. Long ago, she had sold her

soul to him. Now Hades was using Meg to discover

Hercules' weakness. Once he had defeated the strong

man, Hades could wage a war against his enemy, Zeus.

Soon it was clear that Hercules' only weakness was his love for Meg. So Hades captured Meg and bargained with Hercules for her freedom. "Give up your strength for about twenty-four hours—say, the *next* twenty-four hours," Hades said. In the deal, Meg would be set free.

Before he agreed, Hercules made Hades promise that Meg would not be harmed. Then, as he shook hands with the dark lord, his strength slipped away, and a terrible war began.

Under the sea, Hades released the Titans, monsters

of wind, ice, fire, and rock. The Titans marched from their underground prison to battle Zeus. Meanwhile, Hades sent the monster Cyclops to keep Hercules from ruining his plans.

Although Hercules was weak, Phil urged him to

fight back. He believed Hercules could be a hero even without his mighty strength. Determined,

Hercules grabbed a flaming torch and poked the Cyclops in his eye. Then he tied his feet

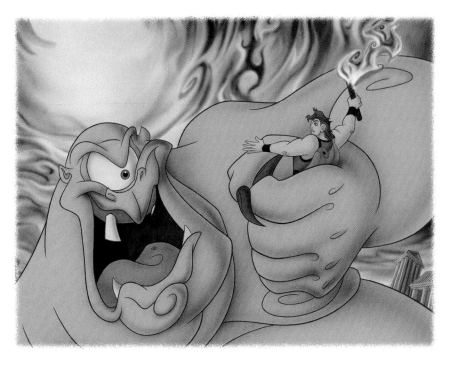

together. As the monster stumbled and fell, it knocked

over a giant column that fell toward Hercules.

"Hercules! Look out!" cried Meg. She pushed him out

of the way and the column fell on her. Meg really did

love Hercules. Her loyalty was to him, not Hades. But she was dying.

In a rage, Hercules flew to defeat Hades. Hades' deal was broken once Meg was hurt, and Hercules' strength returned to him! He broke the chains that were holding the gods and freed his father from his lava-encased prison. Then he grabbed the Tornado Titan. All of the

Titans were sucked into the swirling wind. With one

mighty toss, Hercules threw them up into the stars.

Zeus cheered for his son. But Hercules wasn't

finished yet. He had to save Meg. Racing into the
Underworld, he saw Meg's spirit floating in the Pit of
Souls. As he jumped in and rescued her, a golden light
surrounded Hercules. By risking his life for Meg, he

had become a true hero at last!

Finally, Hercules could return to Olympus. But

he knew that he could not stay there. A life on earth

with Meg was better than an immortal life with the gods. Zeus was so proud, he made a picture of his son in the stars so that everyone would remember the mighty Hercules.